# ESCAPE FROM ...
## Hurricane Katrina

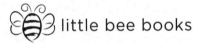 little bee books

New York, NY
Copyright © 2020 by Little Bee Books
All rights reserved, including the right of reproduction
in whole or in part in any form.
Printed in China RRD 0321
littlebeebooks.com

Library of Congress Cataloging-in-Publication Data
is available upon request.
ISBN 978-1-4998-1108-7 (paperback)
First Edition 10 9 8 7 6 5 4 3 2
ISBN 978-1-4998-1168-1 (hardcover)
First Edition 10 9 8 7 6 5 4 3 2 1

For information about special discounts on bulk purchases, please
contact Little Bee Books at sales@littlebeebooks.com.

# ESCAPE FROM...

## Hurricane Katrina

by Judy Allen Dodson
illustrated by Nigel Chilvers

little bee books

# AUGUST 23, 2005

In late August, off the coast of the southeastern Bahamas, a tropical storm is brewing. Warm seawater sparkles in the sunshine. Soon, warm, moist air begins to rise. It's slow at first, like a gentle breeze. But then it starts to speed up. Faster and faster, the air rises and pushes outward. New air is sucked up within this now-swirling wind. The warm air continues rising, forming a column of clouds. Within hours, the spinning cluster of high winds, now joined by thunder and lightning, becomes a full-blown tropical storm. The pounding winds howl, and the sea seems to shake.

The tropical storm spins its way west, crossing

over warm Atlantic waters. The storm uses this heat as fuel, turbocharging itself into a newly formed, and very fierce, hurricane. It's the eleventh tropical storm of the season, and meteorologists from the World Meteorological Organization (or WMO) will soon choose the next name on their alphabetical list for it: Katrina.

Two days later, Hurricane Katrina crashes off the southern Florida coast with Category 1 winds. It's swirling at 85 miles per hour, fast enough to cause damage. The warm waters of the Gulf of Mexico give it more fuel and increases its power. The winds are now furious. They speed at over 125 miles per hour, daring anything to get in its way. Katrina rushes forward toward Louisiana—now a Category 3 hurricane. This is where the low-lying city of New Orleans waits, protected from flooding by miles of concrete levees. But can these walls withstand such a lethal hurricane?

# REALITY CHECK

Hurricanes form over the warm ocean waters near the equator. These tropical cyclones use warm, moist air from the region as fuel. Once cooler air mixes with the warm water, it begins to churn. The warmed air rises, causing huge storm clouds to form. With enough warm water, the cycle will repeat itself, storm clouds will increase, and wind speeds will grow to the degree that a hurricane will form.

Tropical cyclones, typhoons, and hurricanes are all the same type of storm. The only difference is location. "Tropical cyclone" is the general name for these types of storms—we use it for storms that form in the South Pacific and Indian Ocean. Typhoons form over the Northwest Pacific Ocean. And when they form over the Atlantic Ocean and eastern Pacific Ocean, we call them hurricanes.

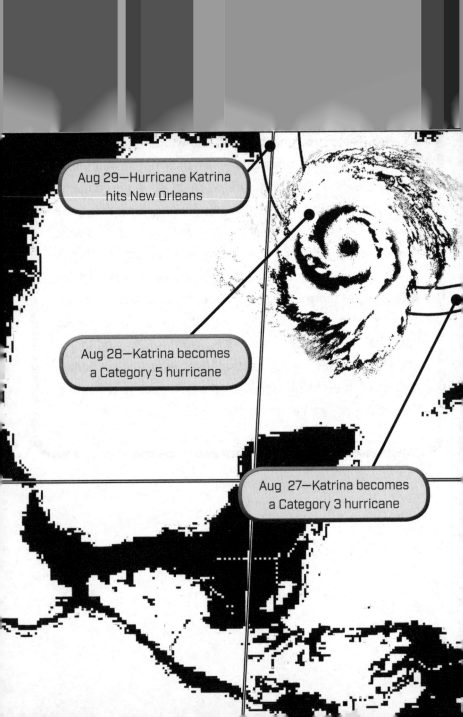

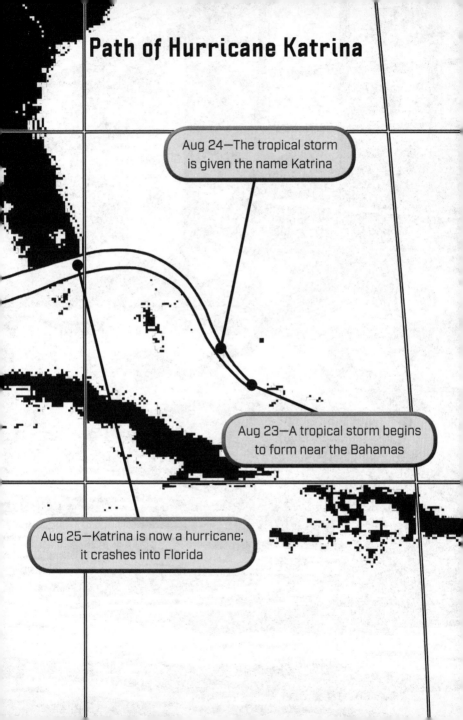

# CHAPTER ONE

# SOPHIE

## Friday, August 26, 2005, 12:00 p.m.

"Swimmers, take your mark. Get set . . ." *BEEP. Splash!*

I dive into the pool, and I can feel my heart pounding in my throat. Even though I'm used to it by now, it's still difficult for me to hold my breath as I take four long strokes underwater. I swallow a gulp of water before coming up for air. I recover, no problem, but I lose valuable time. "Kick, kick, kick!" I chant in my head over and over again with each stroke. My legs slap against the water, heavier and slower than usual, and they don't feel attached to my body. My rhythm is off today. Mama and Daddy aren't here to cheer for me like they have been at my past meets. Mama had to get treatment

7

for her cancer, and Daddy had to stay with her. It feels different without them in the stands.

I'm distracted. "Just swim," I tell myself. "Focus." So what if this is my first sixth-grade swim meet of the season and the girls are bigger and stronger than me? The girl to my right is now ahead of me by a foot, and I panic. I'm losing when I know I can win! Freestyle is my best stroke. I can hear Mama say, "Relax and match your rhythm to Sweet Emma Barrett," as she slaps those piano keys, playing my favorite jazz. Suddenly, my strokes don't feel as choppy and I pick up the pace. My first twenty-five yards are done and I do my flip turn. I've got this. Now I can hear Daddy *tap, tap, tap* tapping his feet to his favorite jazz performer, Charles "Buddy" Bolden. I'm gliding through the water with ease now, my rhythm as smooth and strong as a song. I'm in the flow of the water. Down to the last twenty-five yards, I find my third gear. I take fewer breaths, and cup my hands and pull the water behind me—hard —with each stroke. I sneak a glance to my left, and the girl and I are neck and neck, so I stretch my hand toward the wall and kick as hard and fast as I can.

As my fingers hit the wall, I look up to the scoreboard, and there it is: S. Dupre, first place. My teammates cheer. I snatch off my goggles, jump up and down, and slap the water. I WON! I just wish Mama, Daddy, and my twin brother, Jo Jo, were here to see it.

## REALITY CHECK

*WERE NEW ORLEANS SCHOOLS REALLY IN SESSION DAYS BEFORE HURRICANE KATRINA MADE LANDFALL?*

Yes, students went to school on Friday, August, 26, 2005. It wasn't a normal day, however. All afterschool activities were moved to an earlier time or cancelled. Families knew that *something* was coming, but they didn't know how bad the storm would be. City governments don't like to shut down schools. It forces families to figure out other ways of making sure kids are safe and taken care of. And millions of kids rely on schools for more than just classes. It's a place to get meals and a safe space where kids aren't left alone. We'll never know if closing schools earlier would have resulted in more families evacuating, but we do know it was dangerous for those who stayed.

# CHAPTER TWO

# JO JO

## Friday, August 26, 2005, 3:05 p.m.

For the fourth time this month, Mrs. Taylor gives me a ride home from school. Usually when she picks me up, I'm coming from coding club. But because of the weather, all afterschool clubs got cancelled. Devon says that his mom is happy to do it. After all, Daddy used to give Devon rides home all the time before the Taylors bought a car. Not many of our neighbors have cars, so we help each other out when we can.

Riding home with Devon is cool because we get to talk about the game we're working on for the upcoming design competition on Sunday at the library. We're almost finished. It's a really fun racing game where you have to outrun zombies in randomly generated mazes. We have all sorts of funny obstacles you have to jump over or avoid, like dancing tarantulas and swooping bats. But some of the mazes still have bugs, and not the ones they're supposed to have. They just aren't working right yet. We have some bad lines of code somewhere that we have to find, I guess.

This is the first time in a long time that I've been happy and excited, and not worried about stuff. Like our car, which broke down two months ago and is still in the shop. Or like not having my own laptop to practice my coding skills on. A laptop is too expensive for Mama and Daddy to buy right now. And most of all, I worry about Mama's cancer, which has flipped our life upside down.

The best part of riding with Mrs. Taylor is that she always makes a stop at Rico's Pizza Shack before dropping me off at home. Today is no exception. Devon and I wait in the car as she picks up some pizza and wings for both her family and ours. I know Daddy will protest when he sees that Mrs. Taylor is bringing dinner for us again. But like always, she'll say that she knows Mama's been too weak to do much of anything, and the rest of us could use some help with all we've got on our plates.

"Here you go, boys," says Mrs. Taylor, handing us hot pizza boxes to hold in our laps in the backseat. Devon and I smile at each other. Pizza and video games are our two favorite things.

I'm glad Daddy always caves. I would eat pizza and wings every night of the week if I could! My stomach growls and my mouth waters. I haven't eaten since lunch.

"Ma, can we have just one slice right now?" Devon pleads. "I am HUNGRY!" It's like he's reading my mind.

"Please, Mrs. Taylor? I'm hungry, too."

The very best thing about riding home with Mrs. Taylor is that even though I can tell by the look on her face that she doesn't want us picking over the food before dinner, she's a nice person who can't say no to hungry kids. Like usual, she gives in, and all three of us sit in the parking lot and chomp down on slices of pizza.

Once at home, I set the table for dinner. Even though Mama insisted on staying awake so I could give her a big hug hello, she is too weak and nauseous to eat dinner with us tonight. Daddy is already helping her into bed. It feels weird to set only three places for dinner, but I'm getting used to it, and I'm not sure how to feel about that. Mama had a chemotherapy treatment earlier today, and it usually takes her a day or two before she gets her strength back. Hopefully, I'll be setting four places again tomorrow night.

When me, my twin sister, Sophie, and Daddy sit down at the dinner table, Daddy lets out a big sigh. Turns out, Mama's cancer treatment medicine is costing us a fortune. A laptop suddenly doesn't seem so important anymore.

"Daddy, that means we're over budget for the month already, right?" Sophie asks, and my heart sinks. She's always been quick with math, but I pray she's wrong. It's only the twenty-sixth!

"Yeah, pookie bear, it does. Don't you two worry, though. We'll figure it out," says Daddy. "But let's say an extra prayer of thanks for Mrs. Taylor's generosity tonight."

After dinner, Daddy turns on the news so we can listen while we clean up the kitchen and I finish my chores. It's my job to take out the trash and clean Pickles's litter box. Sophie already fed Jerry, our pet turtle, when she got home from school. We're about to start our homework when Daddy calls us all into the living room.

On TV, a meteorologist is talking about a huge hurricane named Katrina that is only two hours from making landfall on the coast of Florida. It's still pretty far from us, but Sophie and I look at each other nervously. It sounds like it's moving in our direction. We do the twinning thing when we know what each other is thinking.

"Is the hurricane heading our way?" I ask. "I tracked the storm earlier today using mapping software in class. Could its path have changed that fast?"

Daddy doesn't answer, but his frown deepens.

## REALITY CHECK

*WHEN DID RESIDENTS FIND OUT THAT LOUISIANA WAS IN HURRICANE KATRINA'S PATH?*

Meteorologists were able to warn residents that a hurricane was heading toward the Gulf of Mexico [Gulf Coast] by Friday, August 26. This was three days before it hit the state. The tropical storm (which turned into Hurricane Katrina) moved across the Atlantic Ocean from near the west coast of Africa, north of the equator. It first made landfall on the southern tip of Florida. However, as the hurricane traveled further west, it gained more strength from the warm water in the Loop Current, growing larger and wider. Many residents were able to track the storm by watching news reports and listening to the radio.

# CHAPTER THREE

# SOPHIE

## Saturday, August 27, 2005, 10:15 a.m.

"Rise and shine, sleepyhead," a voice says softly from the doorway of my room. I sit up straight as I realize it's Mama's voice. She's out of bed!

"Mama!" I'm practically beaming, I'm so happy to see her out of bed and actually waking *me* up like she used to. "How are you feeling?"

"I slept well last night," she says with a smile. "It helped." She's holding her chest, so I know this isn't easy for her, but she's breathing more easily than yesterday. "And I couldn't wait any longer—I want to hear all about the swim meet! I'm sorry I was too tired to listen much yesterday."

I am happy to oblige, and I give Mama the full rundown. I'm still excited about my first place finish in the freestyle. Mama seems equally excited about the second place I got in the breaststroke. I know I'm getting stronger, too, because after the meet, I still finished my workout at home, which included push-ups, chin-ups, and sit-ups.

"I'm proud of you, sweet pea. I wish I could have been there to see you," Mama says.

"Me, too, Mama." And that's when I finally look at the clock. I must have pressed the SNOOZE button twice and it's my turn to feed Pickles. She must be starving!

When Mama and I walk into the kitchen, the sun is peeking through the curtains and Daddy has already brewed a fresh pot of coffee. Pickles is scratching at her food bowl and meowing, so I feed her right away. Bags from Mitchell's Hardware Store are on the table, which means Daddy has already been out and back. I'm nervous seeing how much he bought because I know money is tight. After last night's news reports of the hurricane hitting Florida, I guess Daddy isn't taking any chances. Jo Jo finally appears in the kitchen (he stayed up late on the phone talking about the storm with Devon and working on their game), and he looks as happy as I am to see Mama out of bed.

"Don't worry about me, babies," Mama says as Jo Jo wraps her in a big hug. "I've already eaten and taken my medication. I've been awake since seven thirty, watching your daddy get things ready for the hurricane. See all these bags?" Mama points to the bags that I can now see are filled with nails, plywood, rope, duct tape, batteries, and all kinds of emergency supplies.

I know what Jo Jo is thinking because, well, we're twins. Daddy wouldn't spend the money unless he needed to. So he must have really *needed* to. I follow Jo Jo into the living room, where he turns on the TV. Sure enough, the local news station is reporting that the hurricane's path now makes it only a couple of days away from making landfall off the Gulf—it looks like it's headed right toward Louisiana!

This house means everything to our family. Me and Jo Jo are the fourth generation to live here on Lamanche Street right off of North Tonti. We're even lucky enough to own the house and the land it's built on, and we'll do everything we can to protect it.

"Mama?" Jo Jo asks with worry in his voice, and I see that Mama is swaying in the doorway. Whether it's from the news or from her exertion this morning, it's tough to tell. But she needs to sit down before she falls and hurts herself.

"Come, Mama," I say as I gently take her arm and lead her back to her room so she can rest. Once she's settled, I return to the kitchen where Jo Jo finishes making breakfast for us. Daddy pops in from outside and grabs a fresh bacon and egg sandwich. He tells us to eat ours and then join him outside once we're done. We need to finish bringing in the lawn furniture, tying down our summertime raft, and securing the windows, and if there's time, helping our neighbors do the same.

Around 4 p.m., I run right smack into Mr. and Mrs. Demery, our neighbors from three houses down. They used to babysit Jo Jo and me when we were toddlers. We hug each other, and I help them carry the containers of food they're bringing over for our dinner.

Inside, Mama is awake, laughing and dressed for company—she's even wearing a wig and not her usual scarf. The chemo treatments made all of her hair fall out. Daddy is smiling and relaxed, and even Jo Jo is wearing his nicest dress shirt. I'm still in an old T-shirt and some shorts, but as Mama would say, I'll make up for that with my best smile.

"Oh, Mrs. Demery, did you make your gumbo?" I can't help asking. I'm starving from not eating much all day and Mrs. Demery makes the BEST gumbo I've ever had. It's stewed in a big pot with chunks of meat like chicken, crab, shrimp, and sausage, whatever she has on hand. It's thickened with okra and seasoned to perfection. Once finished, she pours the stew over white rice. My mouth waters just thinking about it.

"You know it," Mrs. Demery laughs. "And Mr. Demery made his crawfish étouffée." This dish is made just like gumbo, but with crawfish. We eat the gumbo and étouffée with corn bread bites. Jo Jo and I are beside ourselves with joy. Mr. Demery can really throw down on some étouffée!

After dinner, which is even more delicious and fun than I'd hoped, Jo Jo and Daddy walk the Demerys home while I help Mama shower and dress for bed. I put lotion on Mama's back, and we watch the weather report together. Hurricane Katrina is getting stronger and New Orleans in right in her path. I hope Daddy reminds the Demerys to prepare their house and gather supplies, too.

# REALITY CHECK

*WERE RESIDENTS FEARFUL OF HURRICANE KATRINA BEFORE IT HIT?*
Yes, local citizens were fearful of the storm before it made
landfall in New Orleans. They watched news reports and
tracked the storm's location daily after it left southern
Florida. Some felt they could stay and ride out the storm,
and that it wouldn't be too bad. Many residents had been
through other hurricanes and survived and figured this one
would be the same. On the evening of Saturday, August
27th, the mayor, Ray Nagin, issued a voluntary-evacuation
order: It was left up to the people themselves to decide
whether to stay or leave. The Lower Ninth Ward sits on the
farther side of the city near the mouth of the Mississippi
River, downriver, or below, the rest of the city. New Orleans
is shaped like a crescent moon and is surrounded by water
on three of its sides—north, south, and east. And nearly all
of it lies at or below sea level, and is protected by levees
and other barriers to keep water from flooding the city.

# CHAPTER FOUR

# JO JO

## Sunday, August 28, 2005, 8:15 a.m.

I'm the last one to wake up, which almost never happens, but today, everyone's on edge. Even Pickles. She stares out the kitchen window at the rain and high winds swirling outside. Luckily, we still have electricity. Not as luckily, we heard late last night that my coding competition at the library is canceled because of the storm. Sophie's swim practice, too.

Mama and Sophie sit in the living room watching the news.

"What's for breakfast?" I call out to them. Sophie gives me an eye roll and points to a plate of bacon and eggs sitting on a counter over by the stove. She and I have been trading off cooking ever since Mama got sick, and I made breakfast yesterday.

"I shouldn't have cooked you anything, if that's how you show your gratitude," she says.

I grab the plate and pinch Sophie on her arm as I plop down next to her on the sofa. Mama is with it enough to clear her throat a little too loudly, which means chill out or else we'll be on punishment. But she's not with it enough to tell me to take my food back to the kitchen, so I dig in.

The news is nonstop forecasting about Hurricane Katrina. "This storm is ruining everything," I grumble.

Sophie nods. "I hate being stuck inside."

But, I suddenly realize, we're *not* all inside. "Where's . . . Daddy?" I ask.

"He's getting more supplies at Mitchell's," Mama says. She's about to say more when an emergency alert sounds on the TV. The National Weather Service is issuing their most severe warning to the residents of Southeastern Louisiana and the Mississippi Gulf Coast—which means us.

HURRICANE KATRINA: A CATEGORY 5 HURRICANE

WITH UNPRECEDENTED STRENGTH

Mama frowns. "Of all the times for our car to be in the shop! I'm going to call my sister. Their car's still okay. If they're leaving, maybe we should go with them."

Sophie and I look at each other.

"Why, Mama?" Sophie asks. "Our house is strong enough to protect us, right? Plus, we've survived other storms before."

"Naw, baby, this reminds me of stories my mama told me about Hurricane Betsy back in the sixties. It wouldn't be safe to stay here," says Mama.

Sophie and I are quiet. In the silence, a reporter on TV explains what could happen if a Category 5 hurricane hits New Orleans.

I like lists, so I make a mental list:

1. Wood-frame buildings, like our house—blown away

2. Concrete structures, like our school—severely damaged

3. Windows, like the one right next to me—blown out

4. Entire houses, like the one I'm sitting in—washed away

5. Flying debris—like cars, boats, trees, pieces of buildings, and anything not tied down

I try to picture our car flying through the air. The reporter also says that a Category 5 is the highest level; there is no Category 6 on the Saffir–Simpson scale that rates hurricanes. This translates to near total destruction with wind speeds of at least 157 miles per hour. I can't even imagine winds that strong.

Sophie speaks, and for once, we're not thinking the same thing. "Can't we ride out the storm at home?" she asks. "We'll help Daddy secure the house."

Mama just shakes her head as rain gusts against the window. She looks tired. I know she didn't eat much this morning, and the energy she had yesterday seems to have disappeared. She's so weak, a gust of wind could carry her away.

When Mama finally speaks, it's like she's making a list of our options. I'm glad because I'm doing the same thing. "This is the strongest storm since Hurricane Betsy in nineteen sixty-five to hit New Orleans," she says. "Granddad and Grandma always say that a storm this strong is nothing to mess with. I know they'd also say we should leave and join them in Austin with Great Aunt Jean. Besides, I don't know what will happen to me if I can't get my treatment. Even if our house is okay, the whole city could be without power for a long time and that alone . . ." Mama trails off, but we're all thinking about the end of that sentence: *could kill me.*

Not being able to continue her treatment isn't an option. Sophie and I look at each other, and I know we're thinking the same thing. Mama is right. Sophie nods at me to do the dishes, and as I move to the sink, she gives

Mama a kiss on the cheek and says, "Don't worry. We've got you, Mama." Then she heads upstairs to pack our bags and Mama's.

While I do the dishes, Mama tries to reach Aunt Emma on her cell phone. She finally gets through, but from hearing Mama's side of the conversation, it seems like they can barely hear each other. Soon, Mama hangs up and sighs.

"I think they're coming at one thirty to pick us up. I don't know how we'll all fit, but we'll figure something out. We've got to."

"We will, Mama," I say. But inside, I'm not so sure. Their car is small, and there are eight of us in total. But I don't want to worry Mama more than she already is, so I go to her once I turn off the water. Just then, Daddy knocks on the kitchen window from outside. He looks like he's underwater, the rain is so thick. He gestures at me to join him outside. We have work to do. And not much time.

It's 1:30 p.m. and we're ready to go. Our bags are packed with toiletries, two sets of clothes and an extra pair of shoes per person, snacks, and flashlights. The windows and doors are boarded up, all the family heirlooms stored in the attic, and an extra lock has been placed on the shed. It's eerily quiet outside now. The rain and high winds have stopped.

Right on time, Aunt Emma, Nikki, Alex, and Uncle John pull up in their car, which is as small as I remembered and full of stuff. My heart sinks as I walk out to greet them. There isn't going to be enough room for all of us. Sophie, Mama, and Daddy are close behind, with Daddy supporting Mama.

Aunt Emma gets out of the car and gives each of us a big hug. Uncle John, Nikki, and Alex wave from inside. Aunt Emma nods at Daddy and turns to Mama.

"Sis, I wish we could take all of you—you don't know how much. But this is going to be a long drive and we're already packed in tight." She touches Daddy's shoulder.

"I talked to Jermaine yesterday and we agreed—if the storm got bad, you're going to be the one to come with us. It's too dangerous for you here without medical care. Jermaine will keep Jo Jo and Sophie safe."

Mama is shaking her head no and crying. Sophie and I cling to each other. Because Aunt Emma is right. This is both the hardest and easiest decision for us all to make.

Daddy says, "Family meeting." The four of us huddle together for what might be the last time in a very long time. We don't flip a coin or chose straws to see who gets in the car. Mama must go. So, we say our goodbyes. For now.

We stand close to Mama as she opens her pocket Bible to her favorite verse, the Lord's Prayer. Saying it aloud, she grabs Daddy's hands and looks him right in the eye like she's trying to tell him something important. Me and Sophie hold hands with Mama and Daddy, and we pray for the safety of everyone, those traveling *and* those staying. And then we hug Mama with the biggest, strongest hugs we can.

As Mama drives off with Aunt Emma, almost choking on her sobs, we three try to stand tall on our front lawn. But tears start rolling down Daddy's face. Sophie is also crying, and me, too.

"We'll be okay, kids," says Daddy. "We have each other. And we're not alone." He waves to our neighbors next door, who're looking out their windows.

He's right. Very few people have cars in our neighborhood in Lower Ninth. Like us, they'll have to find another way to get to safety or ride out the storm at home.

We're in it together.

# REALITY CHECK

*DID EVERYONE EVACUATE THE LOWER NINTH WARD?*

No, not everyone. There were many reasons why people didn't evacuate the Ninth Ward before Hurricane Katrina arrived. Over one fourth of the residents in New Orleans lived in poverty, and that percentage is even larger in the Ninth Ward neighborhood. Many people didn't have a car or enough money to leave. Some 112,000 of New Orleans's nearly 500,000 people did not have access to a car. Another reason some stayed is because the storm had knocked out the electricity. This meant no phone, TV, or radio, so many didn't get the warning alerts about the storm. Pets were also not allowed at many of the shelters, and lots of pet-owning residents chose not to leave their animals behind. By nightfall, almost 80 percent of the city's population had evacuated. More than 15,000 had sought shelter in the city's stadium, the Superdome, while tens of thousands of others could do nothing but wait out the storm at home.

CHAPTER FIVE

# SOPHIE

## Later that Sunday, August 28, 2005, 3 p.m.

The house feels empty without Mama here. My heart jumps and my hands tremble the more I think about the storm coming our way. Why am I worried? I shouldn't be. Daddy has always protected us from any danger, like the time Jo Jo got stuck in the tree and Daddy climbed up and carried him down. Or when the roof leaked and water flooded my room—Daddy was there to save the day. But we've never been separated from Mama, except for the day after her cancer surgery, and we missed her then. I guess I'm worried about being separated from her more than anything else right now. Jo Jo is quiet, too. He's usually like a jumping bean, all over the place, but now he's just staring off into space. Seeing him like this pulls me back a bit, and I snap my fingers in front of Jo Jo's face.

"Hey, Jo Jo. Daddy needs us to help him move some stuff to the attic. Let's get our minds off missing Mama." That does the trick. Jo Jo nods, and we head up to the attic arm in arm.

Daddy says we need to move quickly just in case the power goes out. For now, we still have daylight and electricity, but the weather reports tell us the storm is moving ever closer to New Orleans, and there's a chance we could lose electricity for a long time. The rain and wind are nonstop again. Earlier today, the mayor called for a mandatory evacuation of New Orleans. Hopefully, Mama can get away from this storm before it gets too dangerous. Even if the rest of us can't.

We create an assembly line to move bins, which contain every valuable item we own: photo albums, jewelry, books, and clothing, as well as some furniture, to the attic. Daddy lets us put some of our prized possessions up there, too. I choose my swim trophies, doll collection, and fantasy series books. Jo Jo chooses some posters and his sneaker collection. To our surprise, Daddy wants to put Jerry the Turtle in the attic, too!

"Daddy, no. Why can't we keep Jerry with us?" I ask. "Pickles is staying with us."

"If we have to leave, hopefully we'll only be gone a couple of days at the most, and he'll be safest up there. It's different for Pickles. It's safer for her to be with us, or at least be where she can climb trees and hunt. Just remember to put some food and water in Jerry's cage so he doesn't starve."

Jo Jo and I don't like that answer, but we don't argue. Jo Jo climbs halfway up the ladder so I can pass him Jerry's cage and he can hand it up to Daddy.

I'm more worried about Pickles right now. I haven't seen her all day. I've looked all around the house and called for her many times and so has Jo Jo. It's unlike her not to come when we call her. I wonder if she got outside and couldn't get back in the house. She's the smartest Bombay cat I know, but I still worry about her. Jo Jo and I agree that we'll look for her again later once we're done moving stuff to the attic and helping Daddy secure the house.

Just then, Daddy's cell phone rings on the hallway table and we all jump.

"It must be Mama again!" I shout. She's been calling every hour, giving us updates on her location. This is her fifth call.

Jo Jo can't get off the ladder fast enough, so I beat him to the phone. I flip it open.

"Hi, Mama! We're all here. Where are you?" I say, all at once.

Jo Jo jumps off the ladder and tries to snatch the phone out of my hands, but I yank it away. Daddy comes down from the attic to talk to Mama. While he's busy, I see Jo Jo sneak up to the attic and come down with Jerry's cage and put it in his room. I don't say a peep. I want Jerry with us when the storm comes.

"All the traffic on I-10 is going one way out of the city," she says. "Cars are bumper to bumper and moving slow."

"Feeling okay?" Daddy asks.

"Feeling just fine. No motion sickness at all."

"Maybe because you're not moving," Jo Jo jokes.

Mama laughs, and so do we. It is so good to hear Mama's voice.

"Honey, don't forget to put Grandma Josephine's fine china set and your daddy's Vietnam uniform and your Satchmo Armstrong jazz albums in the attic, too," Mama says to Daddy. "We can't lose those treasures if the house floods."

"Yes, dear," Daddy answers. Daddy makes a funny face when he answers Mama. Me and Jo Jo cover our mouths and try to hold in our laughs so Mama won't hear us. For a moment, it's like we're all together again, but then the phone line crackles and it's hard to hear Mama's voice. We can barely make out her words now.

"I'll call back in one hour. Sophie and Jo Jo, be sure to help your daddy and get something to eat. I love you all. Stay safe."

"Bye, honey," says Daddy

"Bye, Mama," we say.

After our call with Mama, Jo Jo makes dinner and I stay with Daddy to finish moving the last bins into the attic. It's getting late and we're all tired. Finally, we're done and not a moment too soon.

Because with a flicker, the lights go out.

## REALITY CHECK

*HOW DID RESIDENTS GET WEATHER UPDATES?*

Severe power outages began on Sunday afternoon, August 28, 2005. Many residents didn't get weather updates about Hurricane Katrina because the high winds toppled power lines and cell towers. Battery-operated radios and charged electronic devices allowed for some residents to track the location of the storm. But with so few options, all that many people could do was find a safe place to shelter until the storm passed.

# CHAPTER SIX

# JO JO

## Sunday evening, August 28, 2005, 8 p.m.

As night falls, the wind howls outside. The storm is moving closer. I can feel it. Daddy turns on our battery-operated radio and the broadcast confirms it, at least from what we can make out. There is so much static that it's hard to hear the updates. There is no cell service and our home phone is dead, too. We have no way to contact anybody, and we haven't talked to Mama in hours. Daddy is worried about the Demerys and the rest of our neighbors still here, but the winds are too high for Daddy to go check on them now. Daddy and I helped prepare the Demerys' house after dinner the other night, so they should be safe at home. We hope.

We'll have to wait until morning to check on everyone. Sophie is out of her mind with worry for Pickles, who still hasn't come home.

I don't know if I'm more tired, scared, or hungry at this moment, but dinner is hot and ready, so I focus on hungry, and call everyone to the table. A big shout-out to Daddy for lighting the house up with candles, because Sophie and I didn't know what to do once the electricity went out. Daddy says grace before we eat, but this time, it's different. He prays for all of our friends, family, and everyone else in the path of Hurricane Katrina to stay safe. Then we pray for Mama's strength while she travels to a safe location and finally, for ourselves.

After dinner, I help Daddy take a few more boxes to the attic, but now we have to use a flashlight to see. In the meantime, also using a flashlight, Sophie looks for Pickles in every corner in the house. In the past when she's afraid, it takes her a while to calm down before she'll come out of her hiding spot. We just hope she's still inside. She's never been out in a hurricane before.

But as I told Sophie, knowing Pickles and her nine lives, she'll come through this storm like a champ! Daddy says we'll look for her in the morning when we go check on everybody else.

It's finally bedtime, and Daddy says it's okay for us to camp out in his room. This is good news, because me and Sophie would be shaking with fear alone in our own rooms. We pull our sleeping bags to the foot of his bed, then click our flashlights off. Daddy falls asleep first. Me and Sophie toss and turn.

"I can't sleep," I finally whisper to Sophie. The wind howls and rain lashes the windows.

"Me, neither," whispers Sophie. "Want to play a game?"

"Nah, that might wake Daddy up."

Sophie nods. Instead, she clicks on her flashlight and pulls out her lifeguarding book and begins to read. She plans to take the test when she gets to high school in three years. I look for something to distract me, too. I whip out my flashlight and turn it on, then I search my backpack to find the map of the possible hurricane paths I plotted out in class on Friday. Danger never looked so close before. We're in the path of a ferocious storm.

## REALITY CHECK

*DID RESIDENTS LOSE POWER DURING HURRICANE KATRINA?*

Yes, many residents began losing power before Hurricane Katrina made landfall near Buras, Louisiana, as a Category 3 storm with 145-mph winds. As the storm moved closer, the weather began to change, bringing high winds and heavy rains, causing power outages across the city and state. The use of power for residents was limited, causing many not to get the necessary storm updates from local and national officials. Hurricane Katrina caused power lines to break and knocked out cell phone towers, causing damage to critical energy systems. Residents were unable to use their phones—landlines or cell—or get electricity to their homes and businesses. On August 29, 2005, 42% of people who utilized electricity in Louisiana, 905,075 out of 2,130,925, had none.

# CHAPTER SEVEN

# SOPHIE

## Early Monday morning, August 29, 2005, 3 a.m.

"Jo Jo, did you hear that?" I whisper, setting aside my book. We are both still wide awake. We can't sleep.

"I think it's the wind blowing outside," says Jo Jo without looking up from his map.

"No, I think I hear Pickles scratching at the door. Can you go with me to check? I'm too scared to go alone."

I grab Jo Jo's arm and pull him with me. We turn our flashlights toward the door, then slowly tiptoe to the kitchen. I quietly pull the keys off the hook and we creep, arm in arm, to the back door. My hands are so shaky that I struggle with the latch on door. Jo Jo looks like he wants to run back to the bedroom. The wind is pounding against the house, and it feels like the roof is going to get torn off. I finally get the locks to turn, then I open the door and stick my head out. The wind hits me immediately and almost rips the door off its hinges. It takes both Jo Jo and I to keep the door from flying away. I can't see a thing but darkness and quick shimmers of rain.

"Pickles?" I call. I nudge Jo Jo to call her, too.

Jo Jo comes closer to the door and sticks his head out.

"Pickles, come here, girl," calls Jo Jo. "Here Pickles, come here, girl."

We're both getting soaked from the driving rain. We wipe the rainwater off our faces and call her again. It's pitch-dark outside and hard to see, especially since Pickles has black fur and the only light we have is our flashlights. Maybe I was just hearing the wind howling, like Jo Jo said. I stick my whole body out the door and call Pickles at the top of my voice just one last time before we decide to close the door.

There she is! Pickles comes running sideways, as the wind is throwing her every which way, and she can barely get to the door. But she makes it! She runs into the house with a loud meow. Jo Jo shuts the door behind her and locks it against the storm. We point our flashlights at our feet and the light lands on her, licking her fur. She's soaking wet and so are we. I scoop her up and give her a big hug, and then Jo Jo joins in.

After we all dry off, we feed Pickles and sneak back into the Daddy's bedroom like we never left. We shut the door, then crawl into our sleeping bags all without waking Daddy up. This time, Jo Jo, Pickles, and I are tired. Pickles lays between me and Jo Jo and shivers herself to sleep as we do our best to warm her up. I pray the worst of the hurricane is over by the time we wake up. Me and Jo Jo fist bump, cover up with our sleeping bags, and then fall asleep.

# REALITY CHECK

*WHAT DID RESIDENTS WHO STAYED
IN THEIR HOMES EXPERIENCE DURING HURRICANE KATRINA?*

Early Monday morning at 6 a.m., Hurricane Katrina passed over New Orleans as a Category 3 storm, with wind gusts of over 125 mph, causing homes to be pushed off their foundations and windows to shatter. Damaging winds ripped siding and rooftops off of houses, uprooted trees, and anything not tied down tightly was blown miles away. Anyone still in their homes would have experienced the howling of the storm and tree limbs and other debris crashing into cars, houses, and windows. It was a terrifying morning that no one would forget.

# CHAPTER EIGHT

# JO JO

## Monday, August 29, 2005, 6:30 a.m.

I wake up to Pickles licking my face and meowing. The power is still out and the room is dark. I grab my flashlight and shine it around the room. Sophie and Daddy are still asleep, and Pickles is scratching at the bedroom door and meowing. She wants out of the room, probably to use the litter box downstairs. I'm torn. I want to let her out because her cries are getting louder and the scratching faster as she's frantic to get out. I don't want her to wake up Sophie and Daddy, but I also don't want her to hide somewhere. I creep over to the door, pick her up, and carry her out of the room, shutting the door quietly behind me. Pickles jumps out of my arms and runs off. It's dark down the hallway. My heart is about to jump out of my chest.

"Here, kitty, kitty. Come here, Pickles," I whisper.

I walk down the hallway toward my bedroom. There's a loud creak and I shine the light toward the noise, but no Pickles. I point the flashlight in every direction, but I don't find her. I snap my fingers several times for her to come to me, but no luck. My feet are glued to the floor and won't move. It's just too dark to hunt for Pickles by myself. That's when I hear what sounds like the roof and siding slowing being ripped off of our house, and I take off running. I sprint back into the bedroom with Sophie and Daddy and pull my sleeping bag over my head. I shut my eyes tight, cover my ears, and curl up into a tight ball. It'll be easier to find Pickles once it's daylight, I tell myself. I'm sure of that. It takes forever, but I finally fall back asleep.

This time when I wake up, it is daylight. At last, I feel safe. I'm relieved to see that Pickles has made her way back between our sleeping bags, but Daddy isn't in bed anymore. I listen carefully, and I think I hear Daddy walking above us in the attic. I don't hear the rain and wind howling anymore. I nudge Sophie to wake her up, but she just moans and turns over.

"Sophie, get up," I say. "I think the hurricane is gone! We've survived! We're safe."

"Oh, good," mumbles Sophie. She doesn't even open her eyes. I leave Sophie and Pickles sleeping on the bedroom floor and head for the kitchen. It's time for me to get something to eat. But when I open the fridge, I remember NO POWER! I'm so happy we listened to Mama and put the milk in the freezer so that it'll last now that the power is out. Just then, I remember that Mama isn't in the house. My heart sinks into my stomach. I'm worried about her. I glance at my watch; it's been twelve hours since we've last talked. I bet she's thinking about us, too. I check the landline, still dead.

We could be out of power for a couple of days with all the rain we've had. I close the fridge door and head over to the pantry to get some bread to make a PB&J sandwich.

Suddenly, my socks and feet are soaked. The pantry is wet! I leap over the wet floor to the edge of the living room and land on the carpet, but even that oozes water. There's also a large puddle in the middle of the living room floor, and puddles in every direction I look. What's going on here? Is there a leak? I search all around for the places it could be coming from. There must be a crack or break in a pipe somewhere. I go to the front door and that's when I see it . . . water is streaming in under the door from outside.

# REALITY CHECK

*What caused homes to flood in the Ninth Ward?*

Just over half of New Orleans lies above sea level. Because of this, a system of levees and seawalls were built by the Army Corps of Engineers to prevent the city from flooding. To the city's east, the levees were weakened by waterlogged swamps and marshes. The low-lying neighborhoods, like St. Bernard Parish and the Ninth Ward, sat below sea level and were at great risk for flooding. These neighborhoods also housed some of the city's poorest and most vulnerable residents. Hurricane Katrina's storm surge grew as high as nearly thirty feet in some places, causing the city's unstable levees and drainage canals to fail. Water seeped through the soil underneath some levees and swept others away altogether. Millions of gallons of water swept in and flooded the low areas, while the historic areas of the city located on higher ground were left relatively unscathed.

# CHAPTER NINE

# SOPHIE

## Monday, August 29, 2005, 9:00 a.m.

"Water! Water!" Jo Jo is yelling downstairs, but I don't understand what he means. I know we have plenty of water now, especially with all the rain. "Of course there's water everywhere," I mumble to Pickles, who stretches out next to me. "We just had a hurricane come through!" Pickles blinks her yellow eyes in what I imagine is agreement.

"Just relax, Jo Jo. You're always overreacting about something."

"Daddy! Sophie! Come down!" Jo Jo yells. "It's an emergency!"

All I want to do is rest, but I get up and meet Daddy

on the stairs, now rushing down from the attic. We hustle to the living room to see what all the commotion is about.

"Daddy, come look," Jo Jo calls. "Water is pouring in from under the front door, come see. The living room is flooded."

I run to get to the living room, and there it is. Water, rushing in under the front door. Our whole living room soaking wet.

"What's going on?" I ask Daddy, trying not to panic. "Why didn't you wake us up?"

Daddy looks stunned. "I . . . I don't know. I've been in the attic repairing a hole in the roof. I checked the entire outside and inside of the house when I woke up. Water wasn't in the house then," says Daddy. He frowns. "This is an emergency, Jo Jo. You're right. Hurry up and get dressed. We have to leave soon. Looks like the levees broke wide open."

Daddy peeks through the boarded-up window and then tries to open the front door with a firm yank. It won't budge. My heart pounding, Jo Jo and I run to our rooms and get dressed as fast as we can. I put on a T-shirt and some jeans. Jo Jo does the same. I slip on a pair of swim shoes. I give Jo Jo a pair, too. We grab our Lawless Junior High School backpacks, the ones we stuffed with supplies yesterday. Jo Jo grabs my arm, and we dash back downstairs.

Daddy meets us at the bottom of the steps and tells us to turn right around. The water is rising fast in the house. Our first floor is already full of water up to Daddy's shins.

"We have to get out of the house NOW!" Daddy yells over the rushing water with a stern warning. "Our best chance to escape is from the second floor."

Daddy wades through the rushing water to reinforce the already boarded-up doors and windows, which slows the incoming water some. Meanwhile, Jo Jo and I run back upstairs to Jo Jo's room. He opens his backpack and jams in a can of white spray paint, Jerry's cage, and some cans of tuna fish for Pickles. I scoop Pickles up and Jo Jo opens his window for us to climb out of using a safety ladder. This is the first time I actually look out the window since I woke up to Jo Jo's yells. Our entire neighborhood is under water. I can see the Demerys out on their front porch waving for help, water sloshing at their feet.

Daddy races up the stairs. He planned ahead and secured the ladder to the house yesterday. Daddy goes first, climbing out the window with a backpack of supplies on his back. Once he gets his footing, I hand him Pickles and they both crawl down together. Pickles is squirming in Daddy's arms, squeamish from all the water surrounding us. I'm next to go. The ladder waves from side to side. Daddy's standing in the moving water, holding the ladder steady at the bottom while Jo Jo grips the top. It's still hard to climb down, and the ladder seems to pull away from the house with each step. How did Daddy get down so easily? This is my first time on this wobbly thing. Daddy yells up for me to put one foot after the other and keep my eyes on the ladder and not the ground. Once I'm down, Daddy gives Pickles to me so he can brace the ladder with both hands for Jo Jo. Pickles is really wiggly now, and it's hard to hold her. She's meowing loudly and scratching me as she tries to climb up my body.

She wrestles her way out of my arms and jumps down into the water. I reach for her, but Daddy stops me before I fall into the rising, waist-deep water. We see her swim over to a tree and climb it. Daddy reassures us she's better off than we are right now.

Jo Jo comes down next, and then we wade through the brownish water, trying to get to the inflatable raft tied down behind our house. It's getting harder and harder to keep our footing as the water rushes between our legs. It creeps me out that I can't see through to the ground like I can in the pool. Anything could be swimming in this water, even an alligator. I'm starting to freak myself out and I slip on something squishy. I try to keep my balance, but it's too late. I land face-first in the water. Luckily, Daddy is there to pick me up. Finally, we make it to the backyard. Daddy lifts Jo Jo and me into the inflatable raft, then tethers it around his waist with a rope and walks next to it.

"Where are we going now, Daddy? And who's going to take care of Pickles while we're gone?" I ask, wiping away tears. Daddy throws his arms around both me and Jo Jo.

"We'll be okay, kids. We're going to higher ground until the water goes down," says Daddy. "And Pickles will be just fine. We've got to worry about ourselves right now."

Still, he pulls the raft under the tree where we wave bye to Pickles. She's hiding and won't come out. There doesn't seem to be much time to get to higher ground, I fear. Daddy pushes the raft toward the street, while Jo Jo and I use the oars to help guide it along the moving water. The floodwater's current is strong. Daddy's grip on the raft and the rope gets tighter.

"Daddy, look! The Demerys!" screams Jo Jo.

"They're trying to get off their porch! I saw them from the window," I say. Daddy nods and we move the raft toward their house.

"Hey, wait there. Don't move," Daddy yells to the Demerys when we get close. "We're coming to get you."

But it's too late, Mr. Demery slips and falls into the water. Mrs. Demery tries to help get him back up on the porch, but she can't lift him. The rushing water is too strong. We use the oars to help Daddy secure the raft next to them. Daddy starts toward Mr. Demery, but the powerful current pulls the raft one way while Daddy's moving toward the Demerys in the other direction. It's too much, even with our paddles. If Daddy's going to save Mr. Demery, he has to let go of the raft. "Save him, Daddy," Jo Jo says. "We'll be safe here in the raft."

Daddy says, "Listen, you can do this, kids. Head to the Superdome. I'll meet you there. You've got this. I'll be there as soon as I can."

Daddy unties the rope from his waist and wades as

fast as he can toward the porch to save Mr. Demery from drowning. The rope slips from Daddy's hands, sending our raft drifting off into the floodwaters.

## REALITY CHECK

*HOW DID RESIDENTS ESCAPE THE FLOODWATERS?*

Tons of water from the breached levees poured into the low-lying neighborhoods. It didn't help that the levees were poorly constructed. Some residents took to the only safe areas in their homes like an attic or a rooftop and waited to be rescued. Others escaped the floodwaters by swimming or taking watercraft through the water to higher ground. By 9 a.m., on Monday, August 29th, flooding began in places like St. Bernard Parish and the Ninth Ward. By Wednesday, August 31, 80 percent of the city was under some quantity of water.

# CHAPTER TEN

# JO JO

## Monday, August 29, 2005, 10:00 a.m.

It takes only a second for panic to set in. But some part of me keeps it together and I yell, "Daddy! How do we get to the Superdome?"

"Which way do we go from here?" Sophie asks.

We can barely hear Daddy yelling over the water churning, "Float to the St. Claude Avenue Bridge. Get across the bridge before the water rises too high, or you won't be able to cross it. You know the way from there. I LOVE YOU BOTH. STAY TOGETHER!"

"I love you, Daddy!" I shout back, tears pooling in my eyes.

"I love you, too, Daddy!" shouts Sophie with her arms stretched out toward him.

First, Mama, then Pickles, and now Daddy are gone.

We're four houses down from our house, beaten yellow now by the hurricane, and two from the Demerys' house. We're just not strong enough to paddle against the current. So, we float alongside cars and other debris. Daddy and the Demerys disappear into their house and a feeling of sadness comes over me.

"We're alone," I say.

"I know," says Sophie. "But at least we're strong swimmers."

She's right. We can survive this.

Our raft keeps us traveling south on Lamanche Street at a fast pace. The floodwaters are strong and getting higher. We know how to get to the bridge because we've been there plenty of times before, but we've never had to do it by ourselves, in a raft, on flooded streets.

Sophie and I sit close to each other in the raft, steering with the oars. I've never seen anything like this before: people on rooftops waiting for someone to save them because their homes, like ours, are flooded up to the ceiling. I wish we could do something, but we are struggling as it is just to keep our raft going in the right direction.

But right before we can get off Lamanche Street, that's when I hear it. Cries for help.

## REALITY CHECK

*How high and fast did the floodwater flow into the Ninth Ward?*

Within hours of Hurricane Katrina's arrival to Louisiana, levees and canal floodwalls were breached. Twenty feet of powerful storm surges from the Gulf of Mexico began flooding communities along the northeastern shore of New Orleans, including the Ninth Ward. The water became trapped inside with no place to go, creating a "bowl" effect. New Orleans would soon be surrounded with floodwater to both the east and west of the canal, from Lake Pontchartrain to the Mississippi River.

# CHAPTER ELEVEN

# SOPHIE

## Monday, August 29, 2005, 11:00 a.m.

"Help us! We can't swim. We have small children."

I see a woman carrying a baby, her husband, and three young kids standing on top of a car all holding tight onto a street sign. Jo Jo looks at me, and all I can see is the face Dad gave us before he let us go. We *have* to save this family.

"We can help them," I say, and Jo Jo nods. If he's afraid, I don't see it in his face. He looks so much different than the crying boy of just an hour ago.

We row against the current to get to them, our muscles burning. Jo Jo ties the rope from the front of the raft to the street sign to steady it. The husband puts his three small children in first, no problem there. They are all soaked to the bone and shivering despite the warm weather. But when the mom hands him the infant, she's slammed by a large, floating branch. It all happens so fast. She loses her footing and has to reach back to re-grab the sign. The motion pulls the baby back slightly toward her, just enough for the child to slip through the outstretched fingers of her husband. And just like a drop of rain, the baby hits the rushing water and disappears.

It's like a nightmare. The mom screams and her husband bends over and frantically churns the water with his fingers. I can't believe this is happening, but I know what to do.

My body moves before I can even think. My hands tie my braids up a split second before I rocket into the water. This is what I've been training for. *I can do this!*

I try to keep my eyes open underwater, but it's so murky that I can't see a thing. It's all just specks of gross, and it burns my eyes. It's nothing like I've ever swam in before. I spread my hands out, searching where I think the baby should be. Nothing.

I have to surface for a quick breath. "Sophie, that way!" Jo Jo calls, pointing somewhere ahead of me. I can hear the panic in his voice.

I don't respond. There's no time. I slip back under the water and kick furiously. Every second now is life or death.

This time, I'm under even longer than before. I know the baby will be pulled away from us by the water quickly, so I have to move fast and far. If I swim with the current, I should be able to make up a lot of ground. I force my eyes open and I kick hard. Shadows cross my vision, but when my hands search them, there's still nothing. The hard swimming has got my lungs aching. I'm running out of air, but I refuse to surface. I can't. For a moment, I think I might pass out, and then a dark blotch passes in front of my eyes. I'm losing oxygen. But then the blotch wiggles, and my heart jumps. I pull through the water with all my strength, reaching out my arm like I'm desperately touching the wall at the end of a race. I inadvertently swallow some water as I stretch out, pushing myself to the limit. And then my fingers wrap around something soft and alive. I pull it to me, kicking my legs hard, and then burst up to the surface. I hold the bundle high above me, treading water with just my legs. With a dramatic cry, the baby is out of the water.

The family is crying, screaming, and pointing to us. We've traveled really far from the raft and are still moving farther. I can't swim and hold the baby up at the same time. But I will never, ever, drop this kid. I accidentally swallow more of this dirty water.

"Jo Jo, hurry!" I yell. "I don't know how much longer I can tread water!"

My lungs are on fire, and I get more water in my mouth. I try to spit it out, but I've got to keep my focus. We're not safe. Not yet.

# REALITY CHECK

*Did people really get caught in the floodwaters?*

Yes. On Monday, August 29, 2005, only hours after Hurricane Katrina made its second landfall, this time in Louisiana, residents in low-lying neighborhoods soon realized that the storm surge waters were rising quickly and flooding their homes. Many tried to escape the violent floodwater by leaving their houses and seeking out higher ground. Once wading through the rushing water became almost impossible, they grabbed onto any standing structures like trees or street signs, or any floating debris they could find to save their lives. Meanwhile, those who stayed in their homes took refuge in attics and cut holes in their rooftops for ventilation and waited for help.

# CHAPTER TWELVE

# JO JO

## Monday, August 29, 2005, 11:30 a.m.

"Get in the raft and untie the rope!" I yell to the dad as I hand Sophie's oar to the mom. "Paddle now!" I direct her as we break free from the sign.

We cover ground fast, but Sophie and the baby are half a block away and still moving. I don't know how, but in between breaths, I manage to keep barking orders. I look to the dad and tell him, "You're going to have to catch my sister and your baby and pull them all in the boat at the same time."

He nods at me, and he no longer looks afraid. He rolls up his shirt sleeves, exposing his skin. This way, Sophie has something to hold onto, his arms. If she accidentally grabbed his shirt instead, it could tear away and we'd lose her.

The mom tells her kids to get to the far side of the raft. It will keep the weight balanced when we have to pull them in. It's smart thinking. If we topple the raft, we're all in trouble.

As we get close to Sophie, I paddle hard against the current. I've got to slow the raft down as much as possible. My muscles are straining, and my heart is beating out of my chest. Miraculously, we've slowed the raft down a lot. The dad is able to reach out and grab Sophie. And with all his strength, he pulls Sophie, holding the baby, into the raft.

Everyone is exhausted. Half the raft is crying, and everyone is hugging. The baby is crying the loudest, but it's safe now in her mother's arms. I drop my oar into the raft and hold onto my sister tighter than I've ever held anyone.

"It's a miracle, Sophie. You saved the baby!" I can't believe it. My sister is a hero. "You did it! You saved her!" The family is sobbing and so am I.

Between coughs, Sophie smiles weakly. "What, you didn't think I could?"

I laugh. "I never doubted you, but you scared me on your second dive down. You were down there much longer that time. What happened?"

"It scared me, too," Sophie admitted. "The current took the baby with it, so I had to get deeper and farther away from the raft. I swallowed a lot of water, too. But I got skills, right?"

"Yeah, yeah, whatever. Mama and Daddy would be proud of you."

Sophie laughs between coughs, then lies down. She's still trying to catch her breath. It's so hot and humid today, we all drink some bottled water from our backpacks to cool off. The family thanks Sophie with hugs. I resume directing the raft again, and we continue toward the St. Claude Avenue Bridge, seeking higher ground like Daddy told us to do.

# REALITY CHECK

*WHAT WAS THE TEMPERATURE AFTER
HURRICANE KATRINA PASSED THROUGH NEW ORLEANS?*

By early afternoon, on Monday, August 29, 2005, the tail end of the storm moved north from Louisiana toward Mississippi, leaving behind a trail of destruction. The dark, cloudy skies with warm and humid temperatures in the upper 80s became a problem for stranded residents. With no fresh water to drink or electricity, and floodwaters continuing to rise, hurricane survivors became dehydrated quickly and became sick from the heat and lack of nourishment.

# CHAPTER THIRTEEN

# SOPHIE

## Monday, August 29, 2005, 2 p.m.

After our rough and wild ride through the floodwaters, we finally make it to higher ground. Daddy was right. Taking the St. Claude Avenue Bridge was the best way. I can't wait to tell Mama and Daddy that I saved a baby. And who knew Jo Jo could steer the raft better than anyone? They will be so proud of both of us.

We say goodbye to the family we helped. They thank us for being good kids and for the ride. They're going to the Superdome for shelter, too, but Jo Jo tells them to go on without us because they're eager to set off and get their baby checked out by a doctor after her ordeal. I'm relieved now to be in water that's only up to my waist and not to my chest anymore. Once the family leave, we take stock of our remaining supplies. They're a little wet, but we didn't lose anything. Flashlights, PB&J sandwiches, a few water bottles, a can of spray paint, toothbrushes, hairbrush and comb, and a small blanket. With a silent prayer of thanks, I help Jo Jo push the raft back into the floodwaters. I hope it will find some other person to help. It saved all of our lives.

I can't help thinking about all of the people who are still stuck. Who didn't have a raft. Who can't swim. I wish we could have helped more of them get to safety, but we did our best.

Now, we have to wade the rest of the way to the Superdome. As we go, I keep thinking about our neighbors on rooftops waiting to be rescued. I start to cry. I see Jo Jo wiping away tears, too, so I'm pretty sure he's thinking the same thing I am. We're really lucky and so many others haven't been nearly as fortunate.

We haven't even gone half a block, and suddenly I'm feeling overcome by the heat. About thirty minutes later, my head is really pounding. I can barely stand up without Jo Jo's help. It's been a couple hours since I swallowed all that water, and I'm pretty sure it wasn't good for me. Too much gross floating in it. My stomach doesn't feel so good, and this heat and humidity aren't helping. It must be about dinnertime and somehow it feels hotter than it did only an hour ago.

I'm worried that I'm not going to be able to make it to the Superdome without getting sick. Jo Jo tries to help me walk, and some people we encounter are kind enough to give us directions when it seems we've gone off course. But there are some mean people around, too. We stay away from the people who don't look friendly. Mama always says if you see crazy folks walking toward you, honey, cross the street. We've been doing a lot of crossing the street since we've been on higher ground. Jo Jo jokes and tries to cheer me up. He says that we'll have lots of stories to tell once this is all over. I give him a weak smile, and then I finally get sick. What little food I ate this morning is now floating in the floodwater.

Jo Jo looks worried and keeps trying to get me to drink water. With the way I'm feeling now, I doubt we'll make it to the Superdome in time to meet Daddy. I don't even know if I can take another step.

## REALITY CHECK

*DID PEOPLE GET SICK FROM THE FLOODWATERS?*

Yes. The floodwater was filled with sewage, dirt, dead bodies, debris, and oil, among other things. Many evacuees who came in contact with floodwater did get sick. The way Hurricane Katrina filled New Orleans with contaminated floodwater made the city a unique toxic dump site. And with thousands of homes already six- to nine-feet deep in the floodwater, the city would stay that way for days until the water was finally pumped out.

# CHAPTER FOURTEEN

# JO JO

## Monday, August 29, 2005, 4:30 p.m.

"Sophie. Sophie! Wake up."

I can't get Sophie to open her eyes. She fell down and collapsed right in my arms. I barely caught her in time before she fell into the water. I drag Sophie and stand her up against a nearby building. She hasn't been feeling good, but she was walking and talking just a few minutes ago. Now her eyes are closed, and she's not answering or responsive. This is not good, and I can feel myself starting to panic. I can't lose Sophie, too. I put my face close to hers, and I can hear she's still breathing. Thank goodness! I pat her face and yell her name.

"S O P H I E!"

"S O P H I E!"

"S O P H I E!"

No answer.

"Come on, Sophie! Get up!"

I don't know what to do without Sophie, even if she's always bossing me around. But most of the time, I kind of love that she's in charge. She knows what to do when things get hard. I take a deep breath. What would Sophie do? I must get somebody to help her. Can I leave her here on the curb? No, I can't do that. But how can I find help if I can't leave her anywhere?

Sweat rolls down my face. I'm hot, scared, tired, and hungry, but none of that matters right now. I keep telling myself not to panic. I tell myself I can help Sophie like I help Mama when she's sick. And I have to get help for Sophie if I'm going to get her to the Superdome to meet Daddy. I search my backpack and pull out one of my water bottles. We've been using our water on a must-need basis and for emergencies only. This is an emergency.

For the first time, I notice how the streets smell like rotten meat and somehow look even worse. The hurricane slammed this area pretty bad. There are downed trees, the businesses are all closed, and I can hear people crying for help. I grab Sophie under her arms and drag her up the steps of a deserted storefront to protect her from slipping into the floodwaters. We both lean up against the door. People pass by us on the street, a few stopping to giving us what little supplies they have to offer: water, pain medication, small pieces of food. One woman stoops down beside me and Sophie and prays for our safety and then keeps walking on. That's all she has to offer, but it means everything to me.

Everybody out here I see looks scared and hopeless, just like us. Some are needing serious medical attention, too, but most of them are looking for food. I see store and restaurant windows that aren't already smashed get broken out. People go in empty-handed, but come out with supplies and food. There's nobody around to stop them. I know stealing is wrong, but I also know that everyone is hungry and desperate for help. *I am hungry and desperate for help.* I have to get Sophie to the Superdome quickly. There must be supplies and a doctor there.

I pour the water from my last bottle directly on her face. She still doesn't move at all. I hold Sophie in my arms, rocking back and forth and singing her name. Finally, I hear her moan.

". . . Jo Jo."

I pull Sophie closer so I can hear her better, and hold the half bottle of water up to her mouth.

"You woke up! I've got you, Sophie. Here, drink this."

She takes three small sips of water, but then gets sick again. She's trying hard not to cry, but she's obviously in a lot of pain. I force her to drink the remaining water until its gone. She's not happy about it, but she does it anyway. I look in her bag to see if there's anything I can give her to help her. Jackpot! There's some pink medicine that Mama probably tucked into her bag for just-in-case situations, like the one we're in. I pour out one dose. She drinks it and washes it down with one of her bottles of water. The only way I can get her to drink is by offering her small sips again and again.

About ten minutes after she's taken the medicine, she's able to sit up on her own. She even feels like eating a little. We split my PB&J sandwich. While I wait for Sophie to regain the strength to walk, I reach down in my backpack to feed Jerry some turtle food. I wasn't supposed to take him, but there's no way I was going to leave my little buddy to die in the flood. Wobbly but able to stand, Sophie holds my arm and we follow others wading through the floodwaters toward the Superdome. We're still two miles away. I hope we make it.

# REALITY CHECK

*WERE SURVIVORS NEGATIVELY PORTRAYED FOR RAIDING STORES FOR EMERGENCY SUPPLIES?*

Rescue efforts from several state and federal government agencies were *extremely* delayed, leaving residents to fend for themselves in the days after Hurricane Katrina. Stranded locals had nothing to eat or drink and were desperate to survive. People were negatively portrayed by the media for raiding stores to provide for their basic needs, including emergency medical supplies, food, and fresh water. These people needed help and assistance that largely went unnoticed for nearly a week, while others huddled on rooftops, bypasses, and took refuge in intolerable conditions in the Superdome.

# CHAPTER FIFTEEN

# SOPHIE

## Monday, August 29, 2005, 7 p.m.

"I see the top of the Superdome," I gasp. We've been walking for what feels like days, and every step is difficult for me. The medicine Jo Jo gave me helped some, but I can feel it wearing off now.

"Yep, almost there," says Jo Jo. "You can do it. I know you can."

I push myself even harder for the homestretch, just like I do at swim meets. Daddy is probably waiting for us, I tell myself as we get closer. I realize that he didn't have time to say where at the Superdome we should meet, the inside or the outside. Jo Jo is getting excited.

He must be feeling hopeful. I can hear it in his voice, even though he looks tired.

When we arrive at the Superdome, the parking lot is full, but not full of orderly parked cars. I mean, it's full with hundreds and hundreds of sick, grieving, desperate people walking around like zombies. No one seems to have a clue which way to go. Where do we check in or get help? I don't see Daddy, either. My heart sinks again. This can't be happening to us. Jo Jo is still holding me up by my left arm, but then he locks arms with me so we won't get separated in the crowd. We look around, but we don't recognize anyone. This is so frustrating and frightening. We finally made it here, and we're still alone and unsafe.

Finally, after walking around most of the building, we find an area providing help. The line is so long, it wraps around the building and my stomach starts hurting again. I hold back tears and clutch Jo Jo's arm even tighter. How do we find Daddy? We're tired, it'll be dark soon, and we'll need a place to sleep. Jo Jo keeps looking through the crowd and finally, *finally*, he yelps in recognition!

"Devon! Mrs. Taylor!" he shouts. He spots his friend Devon and his family. *Yeeeees!* Devon and his family wave and make their way over to me. We explain how we lost Daddy, and Mrs. Taylor gives us both hugs and tells us to come inside with them. For the first time all day, we're not alone. Heck, we might even be safe.

Cool! At last, we're inside the Superdome! As we enter, we're given a couple bottles of warm water. We hope there might be some food later, but no one seems to know when or where it will be. We've been here many times for Saints games, because Mama and Daddy are big-time fans and get tickets whenever they can. We can get to any section of the seating areas with our eyes closed. I'm finally relieved and feel safe enough to let my guard down. Until we walk up to the 400 Level, that is. An unbearable stench hits us. I get an eerie feeling and immediately get another stomachache. I cover my nose, trying not to smell the foul odor, but it's too late. I clench my stomach. Oh, nooo! I run to the corner and get sick. Everyone's looking at me, but I feel too ill to care. Mrs. Taylor takes her scarf, wipes my mouth, and asks if I'm okay. I know it's okay to cry, but I can't. I must be too dehydrated. I look around for someone to clean up my mess, but there's nobody around to ask. It's not like there are staff members or stadium personnel around. Everyone is just like us. Normal people who have nowhere else to go.

People are laid out all over floor and anywhere else they can find a clear space. I can't believe how many people are here. It looks like thousands. All these people must have heard on the news, like Daddy, to come here for shelter. This is nothing like what we're used to: There are no concessions open for food or attendants to help us find seats, and it looks like the hurricane tore a huge, gaping hole in the roof. Jo Jo gives me a hug and our group continues looking for a place to camp out for the night.

The Taylors finally settle on a place out on the field, close to one of the goal posts. It's dark now, and me and Jo Jo pull our blanket over our heads. We're both worn out and exhausted. Before we go to sleep, Jo Jo shines a light into his backpack and pulls Jerry out. I squeal and reach for him. "I can't believe you had him in your backpack this whole time."

"I couldn't leave him home all alone," says Jo Jo. "I waited until we got to a safe place to surprise you."

I give Jo Jo a long hug. I don't hold back my tears this time. He lets me know that everything will be fine and that Daddy will find us. My stomach pains don't go away. Maybe they'll be gone in the morning. I put Jerry's cage next to me. I'm still praying that Daddy can find us in this big scary place when I fall asleep.

# REALITY CHECK

*Could separated families use their cell phones to locate one another?*

In 2005, many people did have cell phones to talk and text on, but they weren't nearly as common as they are now. It was a much different time. The concept of social media was just beginning, people didn't have much access to it, and even texting was relatively new. Though it seems as if everyone has a cell phone today, this was certainly not the case back then. For those that did have a cell phone, reception and cell service were spotty at best in New Orleans after Katrina. Part of the reason is because cell towers were knocked out after many days of rain and high winds.

# CHAPTER SIXTEEN

# JO JO

## Tuesday, August 30, 2005, 8:30 a.m.

I wake up before Sophie. I see Jerry crawling around in his cage, so I feed him. I see a note from Mrs. Taylor on my blanket telling us that they left to find food and will return soon. Sophie finally wakes up, and she's still feeling sick.

We wait for what seems like forever for the Taylors to return. We get too hungry to wait around any longer, so we leave to search for food ourselves. No luck. We don't find anything after looking on multiple floors and stopping at every concession area. No food, but we hit the jackpot in another way. We spot our school nurse, Mrs. Lyons, on the fifth level by one of the concession areas. One look at Sophie and she knows immediately that Sophie needs medical attention. She places a strip on Sophie's forehead to take her temperature. It's 101 degrees Fahrenheit. She gives Sophie some antibiotic pills to take immediately, and then two more for tomorrow. "I wish I had more to give you, but these are all I have," she says. "I know it's crazy here, but you need to find a doctor as soon as you can. Where are your parents?" She asks.

"We're with the Taylors," I tell her, and she nods.

"Good. Stay with an adult, Jo Jo, it's not safe in here. People are scared and hungry, and there's nowhere else to go."

We get pushed out the way by other people needing help from Mrs. Lyons. When we navigate our way back to our campout location, the Taylors aren't there and all of their stuff is now gone. They must have thought we ran off. It's hard not to panic. We've traveled all this way, gone through so much, and the Superdome is almost scarier than the flood. I try to stay brave and positive so Sophie won't worry. She's still very sick and fighting through it like the champ she is, but I guess we're alone again.

We slowly make our way to the arena side in the stands by the Saints' fifty-yard line. In all our years coming to games, this is the closest I've ever been to the fifty-yard line. Sophie feels faint and needs to sit down. I plop down next to her. Normally, I would be excited about being this close to the field, but right now, I wish I was anywhere else. I'm so hungry, I can barely think straight. We only have one can of tuna fish, two bottles of warm water, and half of a smashed PB&J sandwich left. We're not sure how many more days we'll be here, so we need to ration our food. I rummage through my backpack and find the can of white spray paint. I pull it out and shake it. Sophie really isn't doing well—she doesn't even look up to notice it. She doesn't have much energy and seems to be getting worse. She lays her head on my lap and falls asleep again. I need to find a safe place for her and also make sure that Daddy can find us since we can't go looking for him. What if he's in here, but we keep crossing paths and missing each other? I devise a plan to help Daddy find us.

I lift Sophie's head off my lap and lay it on her backpack, covering her up with the blanket so no one can see her. I look at our seat location and memorize it. I take the spray paint and jog down to the field. I spray a picture of a big turtle and the code T1U4R2T3L6E1S4 on one panel near the stadium floor by the fifty-yard line. Daddy taught us how to play this code game when we were five years old in case we ever got lost during a game. We would take a marker and write down, in the largest letters we could, our seat location by the nearest bathroom. Since the field is closest to where our hideout is, I'll use this location. The answer: TURTLES: Section 142, Row 36, Seat 14. *Turtles* is our family code word for emergency. I guess it's because we've always had a pet turtle and it's not a word you see written down often. We've only had to use it once before. It worked then, and I pray it will work this time.

"Hey! Who's gotta turtle in here?" asks a girl about our age, peeking her face under our blanket at Sophie. "I cracked your code."

Sophie and I are startled silent, and then we all three burst out laughing.

"Well, I guess that means you gotta hang out with us," I say, holding up Jerry. The girl beams. For the first time in days, I don't feel scared.

"What's your name?" Sophie says with a smile, and I can tell how hard she's trying not to show that she's in pain.

"My name is Lucette Rose Xavier, but you can call me Luce. I'm happy to comply."

I let Luce know that I think she's a genius for cracking the code that was meant for Daddy to finds us. We spend the day trading stories about how we got here. There's nothing else to do, and even if there was, Sophie doesn't have the energy for it. Luce got separated from her folks and is trying to find them. At least Sophie and I have each other. Luce is all alone and trying to survive. While daylight is still available, we make up some games and find out we have a lot of things in common. She's our age and her family is also native to New Orleans. That's when Luce pulls her hair up into a ponytail to adjust her florescent pink hearing aids. She catches me staring at them.

"Oh, these things in my ears, they give me my superpowers," she says, laughing.

Her hearing aids got wet when she fell in the floodwaters. They recently dried out and thankfully, they still work. We comfort her and promise to help her find her family.

## REALITY CHECK

*WAS THERE ANY MEDICAL STAFF AT THE SUPERDOME TO TREAT PEOPLE'S ILLNESSES?*

Upon entering the Superdome, adults and children were then given two bottles of water a day. The National Guard soldiers handed out box meals and MREs (meals ready to eat) but all food, water, and medical resources were limited and rationed out daily. Sometimes, there wasn't enough food for the amount of people and not enough medical staff was available to treat sick people for minor or major injuries or illnesses. There was no established sick bay, and whatever cots there were had been carried in by the evacuees themselves.

# CHAPTER SEVENTEEN

# SOPHIE

## Wednesday, August 31, 2005, 1:15 p.m.

I can tell the medicine from the nurse is working. My stomach pains are less severe than yesterday, and I can raise my head a little bit without feeling dizzy.

Me, Jo Jo, and Luce have been exploring a little when not hiding under our blankets, but now I can tell they're almost as tired and weak from no food and water as I am from my sickness. The only one in our group who eats well is Jerry. Jo Jo packed enough food for him for two weeks. I don't know what we'll do if Daddy doesn't show up soon. The Superdome is getting scarier every day. It's so hot and humid inside. Someone told us the hole in the roof lets humidity in and traps it inside. The building's plumbing isn't working and that means none of the toilets flush. All of the concession stand food has rotted since the electricity stopped working and no one has showered in days. If I wasn't already sick, the smell here alone would have made me vomit.

"There's too many people here," Luce says. "I think we need to come up with a plan to get out."

"She's right, Sophie," Jo Jo agrees. "It feels like things could get out of control here any minute. I know there have been fights, and we still have to get you to a doctor."

I think about what they're saying for a second and it makes sense. The Superdome, while dry, is almost more dangerous than being outside. "But where would we go?" I ask. "I heard someone say that there was still a few feet of water surrounding the whole building."

Luce scrunches up her brow. "Well, we could try to find another building and hide out until the water dies down. It might not solve everything, but at least we'd get out of this stink. I don't feel safe here anymore."

We must be talking a little too loudly, because an older woman a few rows down motions us to lean closer to her. Fanning herself with a straw Saints cowboy hat, she speaks up. "I've been keeping my eye on you kids. My husband told me that they're gonna be sending some buses around soon to evacuate us."

"Do you know where they're going to take us?" I ask.

"No idea, hon. But when they come, the three of you stick together and get on a bus. Wherever they go, I hope they'll be better prepared than they are here."

Later, once night falls, we take a vote. We come up with two choices.

1. Wake up at first light and make our way to the nearest exit to try to get on a bus.

2. Wait it out for Daddy, no matter what.

The vote is three to zero. We've got to get out of here now.


We fall asleep, but I get startled awake by someone shaking my arm! Peeking from under my blanket, I see a dark shadow. I'm panicked and am ready to dive on the person to save my brother and Luce. I swear I'm halfway to a pounce, when I hear . . .

"Josephine Abbigail Dupre," a man whispers.

"Josiah Abraham Dupre," the man says, turning to look at Jo Jo.

"Daddy?" I sit up, then blink several times to be sure.

"Daddy! I can't believe you found us," says Jo Jo.

We give Daddy a big, long hug. Never, ever wanting to let him go ever again.

"Your code worked. That's the best-drawn turtle anyone has ever spray-painted. I followed it straight here."

We all laugh, even Luce, who's awake now from all the commotion.

Daddy's glad we stayed together after we got separated from him in the floodwaters. We tell him everything that's happened, and he tells us it took him three days to get rescued by helicopter from the rooftop of the Demerys' house. Mr. and Mrs. Demery were taken to the hospital in Houston and hopefully, will recover there.

"We were going to find one of the buses this morning," I say. "Daddy, we got to get out of the Superdome."

Daddy nods. Even though he just got here, he can see it's not fit for living in. We try to head out, and I see that the straw hat lady is already gone. The lines are long. While we wait, Daddy promises Luce he'll help her find her family.

The lines are not very organized, and they are too long with the assembled people making sounds that are becoming deafeningly loud. So many people are hurt, sick, and looking for lost family members. The last of our food is gone and only a few drops of warm water are left in our bottles. I can tell that Daddy is tired, but he keeps our spirits high. He snaps his fingers, claps his hands, and pretends to play the cornet to the beat of hot jazz from his favorite musician, Charles "Buddy" Bolden between the moving lines.

I see Luce turn her hearing aids up higher so she can listen for her parents' voices in the crowd. When the main line breaks into four separate ones, Jo Jo and I help Luce call out her family members' names. I secretly don't think it will work, but I know how scared Luce must feel. Being separated from my own family was horrible. So I yell loud and ask other people in line to help us. I swear, it just must be a day for miracles, because the crowd parts and Luce is nearly tackled by a woman rushing to hug her! It's her mom, followed by the rest of her family. They heard us!

It feels like we are all going to get a happy ending. We found our father, Luce found her family, and we're getting out of the stinking Superdome. But when we get to the front of the line, we find out we can't all ride on the same bus together. Luce's family is going in another direction, to Baton Rouge, while we're going to Texas.

I quickly write down my parents' cell phone numbers and make her promise to call as soon as she gets to Baton Rouge. Then just like that, we're waving good-bye.

I look out the bus window and notice the floodwaters haven't receded much in the past three days since we arrived at the Superdome. In fact, the flood almost looks worse.

"Everything will be okay," Daddy says. "We're all safe."

"What about our house and all of our stuff?" I ask. "What about Pickles!"

"Pickles is a smart cat. Remember, she got out of the floodwater first. I'm sure she's fine. But our stuff? That's long gone," answers Daddy. "Don't worry, though. We'll be okay. Nothing is more important than being back together."

We're all quiet as the bus carries us out on to Highway 10. And shortly thereafter, we're far from the Superdome, New Orleans, and everything we've ever known.

## REALITY CHECK

*WERE FAMILIES REUNITED AGAIN AFTER HURRICANE KATRINA?*
Yes and no. After families fled New Orleans, some returned, but many didn't. The poorest residents were the most severely affected because of the lack of money and resources to either return (those who left) or rebuild (those who stayed).

# CHAPTER EIGHTEEN

# JO JO

## One year later
## Tuesday, August 1, 2006, 11:00 a.m.

I can't believe I'm standing in our yard again, in front of our own house. This is the first time Sophie and I have come home since Hurricane Katrina. We'd been living in Austin, Texas, with our cousins for the past year. Daddy went home six months ago, but couldn't stay in the house because there was black mold and water damage everywhere. He's been staying in a hotel nearby. He also found a new job as a contractor building homes, and when not at work, he's been repairing our house for us, too. Mama has much more energy now that she's cancer-free. She's eager to return to work at the Alvar Library, but it's going to take at least a couple of weeks since the building flooded with about a foot of water. The books, computers, and interior part of the library were all destroyed. She squeezes my hand and smiles at me and Sophie. None of us can believe we're lucky enough to be back here. Daddy's excited for us to see all the hard work he's been doing to repair our house since the flood. The large oak tree is still standing, the one that Pickles climbed up during the storm. Daddy has kept an eye out for Pickles while working on the house, but no luck yet. We're not giving up hope, though. Sophie found an article about a cat that traveled hundreds of miles home after it was lost. Maybe Pickles is just waiting for us all to get back.

Daddy rushes down the front steps to greet us, and sweeps us up into a big family hug, including Jerry, who's in the cage that Sophie's holding. Tears spring to my eyes, and I can see that we're all getting misty.

"Ready?" Daddy asks. Mama nods. Sophie and I smile at each other and nod, too. It's time to enter our new house for the first time since we climbed out the window to escape the floodwaters. Daddy goes first, Mama next, then Sophie and me. It's clean and dry, but very different. There's nice new carpeting and painted walls with a few pictures hanging up and the sweet sounds of jazz from Louis "Satchmo" Armstrong playing. Mama begins to cry again, for real, and Daddy puts his arms around her and buries his face in her hair. Mama's happy though, I can tell. Daddy, too.

Then Sophie and I do that twin thing again where we know exactly what the other one is thinking. Our rooms! We run down the hall to see them. I burst into mine and then freeze.

There's a bed, dresser, even a brand-new pair of sneakers waiting on the floor. But none of it is what I had before. All my old books, clothes, games, and posters are gone. This is my bedroom now, but it feels like a stranger's to me.

Sophie comes to the doorway. "It's all gone, Jo Jo. Mine, too."

I feel myself tearing up again, but from frustration

and anger this time. "It's not fair," I yell. "I want my old room back with all my stuff in it!" I have so many feelings built up inside of me, and it's like I can't hold them back anymore.

Mama and Daddy appear in the doorway, concern on their faces.

"Jo Jo . . ." Mama's voice is reassuring. She puts her arms around me and gives me a long, tight, everything's-gonna-be-alright hug. "We talked about how things would be different once we returned home. I thought you understood what that meant."

"I know it's hard. I'm still getting used to it, too," says Daddy. "We're going to get through this together, I promise."

"I know you said everything was lost, but I still thought maybe we saved something." I look around. No one has anything to say to that.

I know I was foolish to be holding out that hope. Daddy told us everything was destroyed when he first came to see the house. After we got to safety, we heard on the news that the floodwaters reached nearly twenty-feet high when the levees broke. Daddy said our whole house was submerged. He even had to cut a hole in the Demerys' ceiling while he was helping them, to keep from drowning.

Their house is completely gone now. I noticed that when we stood outside. Mr. Demery broke his hip during the floods, and both Mr. and Mrs. Demery are recovering with their daughter in North Carolina. Daddy doesn't think they'll ever return home.

After a few seconds, Sophie sits down next to me. "I understand how you feel, Jo Jo. I didn't really get that it was all gone until I saw my room with different stuff in it."

It makes me feel better knowing that Mama, Daddy, and Sophie get what I'm feeling. Our whole family has been seeing a therapist to talk about what happened. Together, we talk about nightmares we have about the hurricane, how hard it is to adjust to the way our whole city has changed, and everything we saw and went through. Things are just different now. I'm home, but I'll be starting a new school next Wednesday and most of my friends, like Devon and his family, haven't come back to the area yet. We don't even know where the Taylors are or how to reach them.

Just then, Daddy's cell phone rings, catching us all by surprise. It's Luce's father, ready to put her on the line with Sophie and me! We put her on speaker. She's living in Baton Rouge with her parents and grandparents and is hoping to return home in another year or so. They are trying to get a rebuilding grant from the state. She knows we're moving back home today, and her side of the conversation is all excitement and congratulations. It reminds us how lucky we are, even with everything we've lost. Mama and Daddy chime in to say that Luce and her family are welcome to stay with us anytime, for as long as they need.

"Our next sleepover will be much better," says Luce, and we all burst out laughing. "Tell Jerry hello for me."

I'm beginning to think everything really will be okay,

when the miracle I've been waiting for happens. Just as we're hanging up the phone, we all hear a scratching noise at the back door. Could it be? We run to the door, and there she is! PICKLES! Looking skinny and ragged, but otherwise herself. I scoop her up and squeeze her tight. Mama and Daddy rush over to give her pats and kisses, too.

"I can't believe she survived!" I say.

"I can!" Sophie shouts, triumphant. "Just like that article said! I knew you were smart enough to do it, Pickles." Sophie scratches underneath her chin. Pickles closes her eyes and purrs loudly.

"Hey now, Pickles," Daddy laughs. "You could've come home six months ago. I could have used some help rebuilding this house. I guess you were just waiting for your best friends, Jo Jo and Sophie."

It's crazy to think about all that we've been through. We hear about our storm and hurricanes just like it all the time now. People even say that there might be other storms coming through. I even heard on the news that hurricanes like Katrina are getting more frequent and there could be another one in New Orleans. But for now, we're ok. Our whole family folds together, safe in knowing that we'll make it through any storm as long as we have each other.

## REALITY CHECK

*HOW DOES A WARM CLIMATE AFFECT HURRICANE ACTIVITY?* Although scientists are uncertain whether climate change will lead to an increase in the number of hurricanes, warmer ocean temperatures and higher sea levels could intensify their impacts. So, if climate change increases those rates, they'll inadvertently boost the strength of hurricanes.

**Tuesday, August 23, 2005**—A tropical storm that will become Hurricane Katrina begins to form near the Bahamas.

**Wednesday, August 24**—The tropical storm gains strength and is given a name: Katrina.

**Thursday, August 25**—Katrina is now a hurricane. It crashes into Florida's southeastern coast. Its strongest winds are 80 mph.

**Friday, August 26**—Katrina travels across the Gulf of Mexico's warm water, gaining strength. Its wind speed increases to about 100 mph as it heads toward Louisiana.

**Saturday, August 27**—5:00 a.m.: Katrina has winds up to 115 mph. It is classified a Category Three hurricane.

**Sunday, August 28**
　∘ 2:00 a.m.: Katrina's wind strength continues to increase. Now at 145 mph, it is a Category Four hurricane.
　∘ 9:30 a.m.: Mayor Nagin issues an evacuation order for all of New Orleans.
　∘ 11:00 a.m.: Katrina is now one of the most powerful hurricanes to ever form in the Atlantic Ocean. It is a Category Five hurricane with winds as fast as 175 mph.
　∘ 12:00 p.m.: The Superdome opens its doors for residents fleeing the storm.

**Monday, August 29**
　∘ 2:00 a.m.: Hurricane Katrina loses some of its power as it heads toward Louisiana.
　∘ 8:00 a.m.: The eye of the storm passes over eastern New Orleans. By late morning, levees are breaking and water is pouring into the city.
　∘ The storm rips a hole in the roof of the Superdome, which has now lost electricity. Air-conditioning and refrigeration no longer work. A backup generator is able to keep the lights on.

**Tuesday, August 30**—Temperatures climb to the upper 80s inside the Superdome and the humidity level inside spikes. Food rots in hundreds of refrigerators that stopped working. Water pumps no longer work, so neither do the toilets and sinks. The smell is very bad.

**Wednesday, August 31**—Some buses begin to evacuate refugees from the Superdome.

**Thursday, September 1**—Additional buses arrive at the Superdome, taking more survivors out of New Orleans.

**Sunday, September 4**—The last of the over 20,000 people who took shelter in the Superdome from Hurricane Katrina are evacuated.

## FIND OUT MORE

Callery, Sean. *Scholastic Discover More: Hurricane Katrina*. New York City: Scholastic Inc., 2015.

Hoena, Blake. *Hurricane Katrina: An Interactive Modern History Adventure*. North Mankato: Capstone Press, 2014.

Koontz, Robin. *What Was Hurricane Katrina?* New York City: Penguin Workshop, 2015.

Parker Rhodes, Jewell. *Ninth Ward*. New York City: Little, Brown Books for Young Readers, 2012.

Uhlberg, Myron. *A Storm Called Katrina*. Atlanta: Peachtree Publishing Company, 2015.

## SELECTED BIBLIOGRAPHY

Cobb, Vicki. *How Could We Harness a Hurricane?* Boston: Seagrass Press, 2017.

Hoog, Mark and Kim Lemaire. *Letters from Katrina: Stories of Hope and Inspiration*. Fort Collins: Growing Fields Books, 2007.

Treaster, Joseph B. *Hurricane Force: In the Path of America's Deadliest Storms*. New Zealand: Christchurch: Kingfisher, 2007.